***All children have
a great ambition to read
to themselves . . .***

*and a sense of achievement when they can do so.
The* **read it yourself** *series has been devised to
satisfy their ambition. Since many children learn
from the Ladybird Key Words Reading Scheme,
these stories have been based to a large extent
on the Key Words List, and the tales chosen are
those with which children are likely to be familiar.*

*The series can of course be used as
supplementary reading for any reading scheme.
William Tell is intended for children reading up
to Book 5c of the Ladybird Reading Scheme.
The following words are additional to the
vocabulary used at that level –*

William, Tell, lived, Switzerland, shoot,
crossbow, people, best, archers, Walter,
lakes, day, wait, surprise, father, if,
Austria, governor, village, cruel, castle,
even, meetings, didn't, free, new, hat,
pole, bow, past, friends, over, back, last,
year's, were, took, head, die, belt,
frightened, aim, twang, went, knocked, hit,
tie, storm, sick, steer, fled, dead, set,
feasting, their

*A list of other titles at the same level will be
found on the back cover.*

Published by Ladybird Books Ltd Loughborough Leicestershire UK
Ladybird Books Inc Lewiston Maine 04240 USA

William Tell

adapted by Fran Hunia
for easy reading
from the traditional tale
illustrated by Robert Ayton

Ladybird Books

William Tell was a farmer who lived in Switzerland. He was a good man, and was liked by all who knew him.

He liked to shoot with his crossbow, and people said he was one of the best archers in all Switzerland.

William Tell had some children.
Two of them were boys and the
other was a girl. They all liked to
fish in the lakes and play games

with other children. But one of the
boys, Walter, liked best of all to go
out for walks with William Tell and
to see him shoot with his crossbow.

One day Walter said to William Tell, "I want to be a good archer like you, Daddy. Please let me shoot with the crossbow."

"No, Walter," said William Tell. "My crossbow is too big for you. Be a good boy and wait. One day I will make a little crossbow for you."

Walter thanked him and said no more about it.

One afternoon Walter was playing at home with his brother and sister. William Tell walked into the house and said, "Look, Walter. I have a surprise for you."

Walter looked up and saw that his father had a little crossbow. "Is that for me, Daddy?" he asked.

"Yes, Walter," said William Tell. "Come on out and see if you can shoot with it."

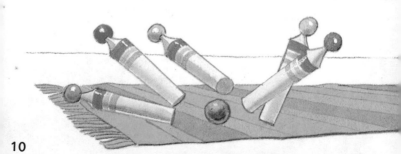

In the days of William Tell, Switzerland was governed by Austria. The governor of Tell's village was a cruel man. No one in the village liked him at all.

The governor wanted a big castle and he made all the people of the village work for him. Even little children had to help.

People in other villages had to work for Austrian governors too. They didn't like the governors and they had meetings to talk about the cruel things the governors did. Some people said they wanted Switzerland to be free from Austria.

15

In one village, a farmer had made a new house. It was a good house and the farmer was pleased with it.

But the governor saw it and
said, "That house is too good for a
farmer. I will not let you live in it."

One day the governor of William Tell's village had his hat put up on top of a pole in the village.

"Tell the people they must stop and bow to my hat as they go past," said the governor to his men. "You are to be here by the pole and see that the people do as I say."

The village people didn't like the governor, and they didn't want to bow to his hat. Some of them went out of their way so that they didn't have to walk past the hat.

After that William Tell and his friends had a meeting by the lake. People from all over Switzerland came to the meeting to talk about the cruel governors.

"We cannot put up with this kind of thing," they said. "What can we do about the governors? How can we make them go back to Austria?"

They talked and talked. At last a man said, ''I know what we can do. Let us wait for New Year's Day. Then the governors will be feasting

in their castles. We can go in and take them by surprise."

"Yes," said the others. "That is what we will do."

Soon after this William Tell was out with Walter. They were talking, and they didn't see the governor's hat as they walked past it.

"Stop!" said the governor's men.
"Stop! You didn't bow to the
governor's hat!"

William Tell stopped, but he
didn't bow to the hat. "I will not
bow to that thing," he said. Then
he walked on.

The governor's men ran after William Tell and stopped him again.

"You must bow to the governor's hat," they said, but William Tell didn't do as they asked.

One of the men ran to get the governor.

"This man will not bow to your hat," he said. "What do you want us to do with him?"

The governor looked at William Tell. "Who are you?" he asked.

"I am William Tell, and this is my boy, Walter," said Tell.

"So you are William Tell," said the governor. "They say you are one of the best archers in all Switzerland." He took out an apple. "Can you shoot this?" he asked.

"Yes," said Tell.

"We will see about that," said the governor. Then he said to Walter, "Go over by that tree, boy."

Walter did as the governor asked. The governor went over to Walter and put the apple on his head. Then he went back to William Tell.

"Now, William Tell," said the governor. "Let me see you shoot that apple."

"No," said Tell. "I will not put my boy in danger."

"The boy is in danger now," said the governor, "for if you do not shoot the apple he will die, and so will you. But if you can hit the apple, I will let you and the boy go free."

William Tell took two arrows. He
put one in his crossbow and the
other in his belt. He looked at
Walter and then at the governor.
"Please do not make me do this,'
he said.

But Walter was not frightened. "Go on, Daddy," he said. "I know you can do it. Let the governor see what a good archer you are."

William Tell took aim. Twang
went the arrow. It knocked the
apple off Walter's head. Walter
took the apple with the arrow in it
to the governor.

"You saw my Daddy shoot the apple," said Walter. "Now can we go free?"

"Wait," said the governor. "You took two arrows, Tell. One was to shoot the apple with. What was the other arrow for?"

"That one was for you," said William Tell. "If I had hit my boy with one arrow, I was going to shoot you with the other one."

"Men!" said the governor. "Tie William Tell up! Put him in the boat and we will take him to my castle."

Walter ran home. The governor's men tied William Tell up and took

him down to the lake. They put him
in the governor's boat and steered
it out into the lake.

Soon a storm came up. The boat
and all the men in it were in danger.

The governor and his men were frightened of the storm. The boat was going up and down, and soon they were all sick.

"There is one man in this boat who can steer us back in this storm," said the governor's men.

"William Tell can do it. We must let him go so that he can help."

William Tell was tied up. The governor didn't want to let him go, but he was sick and frightened too. At last he said, "Let Tell go, then. He can steer us back."

The governor's men let William Tell go and he steered the boat back over the lake. As soon as they stopped, Tell took up his crossbow and jumped out of the boat. He ran up into the hills. The governor and his men were too sick to go after him.

William Tell knew which way the governor had to go to get back to his castle. All he had to do was to sit and wait for him to go past.

He waited and waited.

At last he saw some men going
past. It was the cruel governor
with his men. William Tell took
the arrow from his belt and put it
in his crossbow.

William Tell took aim. Twang went the arrow, and the cruel governor fell from his horse.

"Tell's arrow!" he said as he died.

The governor's men were too frightened to go and look for William Tell. They didn't even stop to see if the governor was dead. They fled back to the village.

William Tell was soon on his way home again.

Walter Tell was at home looking out of the window. He saw a man coming to the house. He looked at the man again and again. Then he jumped up and ran to let him in.

"Daddy, Daddy," said Walter. "How did you get away from the governor?"

All William Tell's friends came to see him. They all wanted to know how he had got away.

At last William Tell said, "I have good news for you. The cruel governor is dead. Now we must make all of Switzerland free."

William Tell and his friends waited for New Year's Day to come. Then people from all over Switzerland set fire to the governors' castles. The governors

were taken by surprise. Some of
them died in the fires, and others
fled back to Austria.

Switzerland was free at last.